Night Fun

Patricia Quinlan   Ron Berg

Annick Press Ltd. • Toronto • New York

©1997 Patricia Quinlan (text)
©1997 Ron Berg (art)
Designed by Sheryl Shapiro.

Annick Press Ltd.

Annick Press gratefully acknowledges the support of the Canada Council and the Ontario Arts Council.

Canadian Cataloguing in Publication Data
Quinlan, Patricia
     Night fun

ISBN 1-55037-487-7

1. Nursery rhymes, Canadian (English).* I. Berg, Ron.
II. Title.

PS8583.U345N5 1996   jC811'.54   C96-930225-8
PZ8.3.Q4194Ni 1996

The art in this book was rendered in mixed media.
The text was typeset in Veljovic Medium.

Distributed in Canada by: Published in the U.S.A. by Annick Press (U.S.) Ltd.
Firefly Books Ltd.   Distributed in the U.S.A. by:
3680 Victoria Park Avenue   Firefly Books (U.S.) Inc.
Willowdale, ON   P.O. Box 1338
M2H 3K1   Ellicott Station
                                   Buffalo, NY 14205

Printed on acid-free paper.

Printed and bound in Canada by
Friesens, Altona, Manitoba.

As a child, my favourite nursery rhyme was this version of "Hey, Diddle, Diddle".
Sharing this rhyme with my own child inspired the writing of *Night Fun*.
I dedicate this book with love to my son, Kevin, who brings such great joy and fun to my life.

–Patricia Quinlan

Hey diddle, diddle
The cat and the fiddle,
The cow jumped over the moon;
The little dog laughed
To see such fun,
And the dish ran away with the spoon.

Two voices whisper down the hall;

Grown-up voices, talking small.

Mom and Dad tiptoe away.

"At last, he's off to sleep," they say.

Though nighttime shadows slowly creep,

Kevin is not yet asleep.

Voices circle round his head

As he lies listening snug in bed.

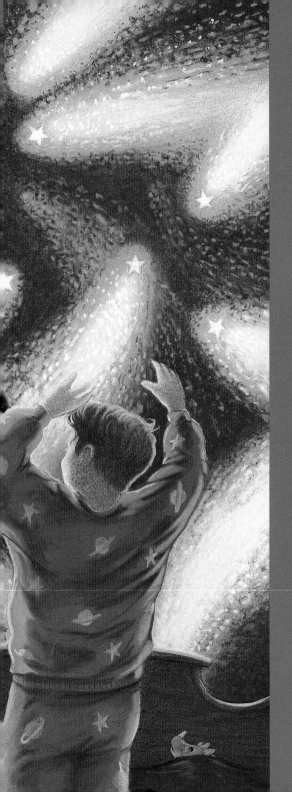

The cow says, "Climb up on my back."

The cat says, "You don't need to pack."

The dog says, "Stars and planets call.

Come on, Kevin, we'll see them all."

Soon Kevin, clinging to the cow,

yells, "I want to take off now."

She cries, "Make sure you hang on tight,"

and leaps into the starry night.

The cow says, "See the earth's blue swirl."

The cat says, "Through dry seas I'll twirl."

"These rocks and earth-rocks look the same,"

says Kevin. "Want a moon-catch game?"

They play until the tired moon

no longer seems so bright.

"Go home," begs Moon. "Oh no," they shout.

"We want more fun tonight!"

They ride across the dark, hushed sky.

Past Mars and Jupiter they fly.

Asteroids go floating by

Until they come to Saturn.

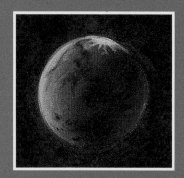

The cow says, "Watch me jump those moons."

The fiddle plays his wild dance tunes.

The cat creates a great Rat King

And Kevin says, "Let's slide down rings!"

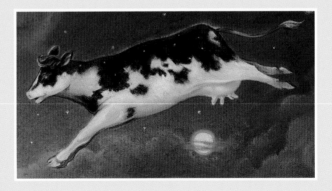

They slip and slide down icy rings
with wonder and delight.
"Go home," begs Saturn. "No," they shout.
"We want more fun tonight!"

They ride across the dark, hushed sky.

Past two more planets on they fly.

They count the comets shooting by

Until they come to Pluto.

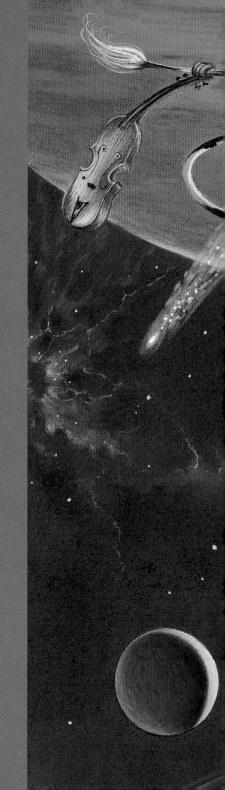

Kevin says, "I'm hungry now."

"Let's have a party," says the cow.

"Fiddle, please sing to set the mood

while Dish and Spoon prepare the food."

They drink star juice and eat moon pie

And rest from their long flight.

"Go home," begs Pluto. "No," they shout.

"We want more fun tonight!"

"On to distant worlds!" they cry.

Again Cow leaps into the sky.

Across the galaxies they fly,

Till Kevin hears a whisper.

A voice inside says, "Come back home.

On other nights with friends you'll roam.

The sun has chased the stars away—

It's time to rise and play all day."